ADVENTURES OF PIDDLE DIDDLE, THE WIDDLE PENGUIN

Piddle Diddle, the Widdle Penguin

and the

SYNCHRONOUS FIREFLIES OF THE GREAT SMOKY MOUNTAINS

Written by Wayne A. Major
Co-Author Ralphine Major

Illustrated by Teresa Wilkerson

Piddle Diddle, the Widdle Penguin, and the Synchronous Fireflies of the Great Smoky Mountains

Written by Wayne A. Major and Co-Author Ralphine Major
Illustrated by Teresa Wilkerson
Book design by Tara Sizemore
Published April 2022
Skippy Creek
Imprint of Jan-Carol Publishing, Inc

Copyright © Wayne A. Major and Ralphine Major
ISBN: 978-1-954978-42-3
Library of Congress Control Number: 2022935943

You may contact the publisher:
Jan-Carol Publishing, Inc
PO Box 701
Johnson City, TN 37605
publisher@jancarolpublishing.com
www.jancarolpublishing.com

Jan-Carol
Publishing, Inc
"every story needs a book"

Synchronous fireflies are one of nature's most spectacular shows. It is hard to imagine that thousands of the fireflies can all light up at the same time and then go dim all together. Because people are so fascinated by this natural wonder, they come from all over the world to see the amazing display that occurs only once a year for a few days.

—Wayne A. Major

This book is in memory of our late father, Ralph O. Major, who passed away in 1994.
Ralph was a dairy farmer who taught us to love and respect animals.

We also write this book to honor our mother, Juanita D. Major, who has been
an inspiration to us as she works to help us bring our trademark character,
Piddle Diddle, the Widdle Penguin, into the hearts and homes
of children and everyone who loves penguins!
We hope Piddle Diddle, the Widdle Penguin,
brings a smile to your face and joy to your heart!

"But Jesus called them unto him, and said, suffer little children to come unto me,
and forbid them not: for of such is the kingdom of God."
Luke 18:16 (KJV)

Piddle Diddle clapped her flippers.
"I'M SO EXCITED!" she said.
Her family won tickets to see the famous synchronous
fireflies in Elkmont near Gatlinburg, Tennessee.

"How much longer 'till we get there?" Piddle Diddle asked.

"We have to drive through Pigeon Forge to get to
Gatlinburg," Mother Diddle answered.

The Diddles could not believe all the shops and motels that were on the parkway in Pigeon Forge.

"Piddle Diddle and I will be doing some shopping for sure!" Mother Diddle exclaimed.

"This road we are traveling on now is called the Spur.
Once we come to the end of it,
we will be in Gatlinburg," Papa Diddle said.

"Piddle Diddle," Mother Diddle called out. "Did you and
Petey know that more people visit the Great Smoky
Mountains than any other park in the United States?"

"WOW!" Petey exclaimed.

"Why are they called the Smoky Mountains?"
Piddle Diddle asked.

"They are called the *Smoky* Mountains because of the fog
that hangs over the mountain peaks," Papa Diddle answered.
"Sometimes they are called the 'Smokies' for short.
We will be seeing the fireflies on the Tennessee side of the
Smokies, but the park goes all the way over into the
State of North Carolina," he added.

"LOOK!" shouted Piddle Diddle. "See the black mother bear
and her two cubs. I'm glad that we are in our car!"

"We want to buy some T-shirts
before our vacation is over," Petey said.

Piddle Diddle loved the idea of going shopping.
"I want a T-shirt, too!" she said.

"We'll come back and shop after we check in at the
motel," Mother Diddle told the excited youngsters.

"I BET THIS FOOD WILL BE DELICIOUS!"
said Mother Diddle.

"I CAN'T WAIT TO SEE THE FIREFLIES!"
Piddle Diddle squealed.

"The synchronous fireflies viewing is a huge
event in Gatlinburg during late spring," Papa Diddle
told the family. "In the summer, there is a Fourth of July
Parade. It starts at midnight and is the very first one in
the nation every year. Then, in the winter they have the
Gatlinburg Fantasy of Lights Christmas Parade. Thousands
of people come to see the parades in Gatlinburg."

Piddle Diddle imagined the thousands of
sparkling lights and shiny Christmas decorations
lining the streets and gift shops.

"Stop, Piddle Diddle!" Mother Diddle yelled while trying to get off the trolley. "Our family has to stay together in this big crowd of people."

As Piddle Diddle came running back, she asked, "Why are they called synchronous fireflies?"

"Synchronous means the fireflies light up all at the same time," Papa Diddle answered. "Then they will all go dim at the same time," he added.

"I CAN'T WAIT TO SEE THE FIREFLIES LIGHT UP THE SKY!" Piddle Diddle said with a big smile on her face.

TROLLEY STOP

"Remember, we must keep the flashlights pointed toward the ground and turn them off once we get to the viewing area," Papa Diddle instructed.

"Elkmont is a very special place," Mother Diddle told Piddle Diddle and Petey. "It has the largest campground in the Smokies. Way back in the late 1800s, it used to be a huge logging camp."

"WOW! That's over one hundred years ago!"
Petey chimed in.

"Yes," Mother Diddled replied. "Some of the cabins and other buildings are still there."

ZIP, ZIP, ZIP!

The synchronous fireflies began their magical show
lighting up the night sky at Elkmont.

OOOHS AND AAAHS were the only sounds
that could be heard from the crowd.

"LOOK AT THE STARS!"
Piddle Diddle exclaimed.
"Where did the fireflies go?" she asked.

"Don't worry," Mother Diddle told her.
"Just watch. They will light up again soon."

"With a little luck, I may have gotten a great picture of the synchronous fireflies," Piddle Diddle said with a big grin.

ZIP, ZIP, ZIP!

The fireflies once again light up the night sky,
and once again
OOOHS AND AAAHS
come from the crowd.

"I'm so glad we came to see these amazing synchronous fireflies," Mother Diddle said.

"Me too!" Petey agreed.

"THEY MAKE THE SKY LOOK SO PRETTY!" Piddle Diddle added.

"It is AWESOME how the synchronous fireflies
can turn off their lights for a few seconds,
then light back up again—
all of them at the same time!"
Papa Diddle marveled.

Piddle Diddle and Petey spread their flippers
back and forth acting like the fireflies.
"We're synchronous fireflies,"
Piddle Diddle giggled.

"It was SO MUCH FUN to see the synchronous fireflies!" Piddle Diddle exclaimed. "Don't forget! We have to get our T-shirts tomorrow," she added as the Diddle family was driving from the parking lot.

With a big grin on her face Piddle Diddle announced the family's next trip, "I WANT TO COME BACK TO GATLINBURG TO SEE THE CHRISTMAS PARADE!"

Piddle Diddle, the Widdle Penguin,
and the
SYNCHRONOUS FIREFLIES
OF THE GREAT SMOKY MOUNTAINS

Tennessee

Pigeon Forge
Gatlinburg
Elkmont

Great Smoky Mountains
National Park

North Carolina

QUESTIONS AFTER THE STORY

Do you remember?

1. Where in the Smokies did the Diddle family go to watch the fireflies?

2. What kind of fireflies were at Elkmont?

3. What are synchronous fireflies?

4. What time of year did the synchronous firefly event take place?

5. What was the name of the national park the Diddles visited to see the synchronous fireflies?

6. What city in Tennessee has the first Fourth of July Parade in the nation every year?

7. In what two states are the Great Smoky Mountains located?

Answers:

1. Elkmont
2. synchronous
3. fireflies that light up at the same time and go dim at the same time
4. late spring
5. Great Smoky Mountains
6. Gatlinburg
7. Tennessee and North Carolina

Wayne A. Major and Ralphine Major

Special thanks to Ivan and Jane Harmon, Annie's owners, for letting Annie appear in our books. Annie lives at Cumberland Springs Ranch. Photo by Steve Ellis of Light House Studio.

Wayne A. Major and Ralphine Major both grew up in Corryton on their family's dairy farm in rural East Tennessee. Always surrounded by lots of animals, they developed a love for them at an early age. Both went on to graduate from The University of Tennessee with degrees in Business Administration. Wayne majored in Marketing and is retired from the State of Tennessee. Ralphine majored in Office Administration with teaching certification and is retired from the Tennessee Valley Authority. Though she has never had a journalism class, she uses her God-given talent as a contributing writer of a weekly true, human-interest column for *The Knoxville Focus* (www.knoxfocus.com).

Years later, one Sunday morning Wayne was sitting in the choir at Wallace Memorial Baptist Church in Knoxville, Tennessee, and something unexpected happened. He was listening to a sermon about David and Goliath that was directed toward the youth. Wayne heard a voice say, "You need to write children's books." He even turned to see where the voice came from. After hearing his story, Ralphine committed to the project as well. While the brother/sister duo had helped teach kindergarten classes at church and admired the children's eagerness and willingness to learn, this was a new venture and a step of faith.

Getting published did not happen overnight, but it was worth the wait getting to work with Publisher Janie Jessee, Graphic Designer Tara Sizemore, and the staff of Jan-Carol Publishing, Inc. The authors believe the great chemistry they have with Illustrator Teresa Wilkerson is because she grew up on a dairy farm in East Tennessee also.

Wayne and Ralphine Major with turkeys on their family's dairy farm in the sixties. Photo by their mother, Juanita D. Major.

Wayne created the character, Piddle Diddle, the Widdle Penguin, which is a registered trademark. Ralphine vividly remembers how excited Wayne was when he shared about hearing a voice that Sunday morning in the church choir. She is happy to be a part of this adventure with Wayne and remembers well that Sunday night when they first talked about this journey that started in the church choir! The authors are proud to partner with two generous donors who have helped to put hundreds of books in the hands of children. God does work in mysterious ways! Throughout this process, Wayne and Ralphine have felt God's hand guiding them and realize how important it is to wait on God's timing. They hold firm to Proverbs 3:6 (KJV): "In all thy ways acknowledge him, and he shall direct thy paths."

Read more at majorbooksofjoy.com and on Facebook

ABOUT THE ILLUSTRATOR

Teresa Wilkerson is pictured with Dora and Tater Bug. Photo by Samantha Brooke Ramsey.

Teresa Wilkerson

Teresa Wilkerson grew up on a dairy farm in Greene County in Upper East Tennessee. She still resides in rural Greene County. Art has always been a part of her life, including the venues of portraiture, murals, backdrops, traditional painting, drawing, and various other art forms. Illustration, especially in the area of children's books, is now her primary focus in artistic endeavors. She finds great joy in drawing stories for children. Visit her website at teresajwilkerson.wix.com/illustrativedesign.

Other Books in the Series:

CPSIA information can be obtained
at www.ICGtesting.com
Printed in the USA
JSHW011345270722
28605JS00002B/4